KARSON DICKINSON

My Heart an Open Wound

An anthology on love, relationships, and mental illness

To my younger self.
You are capable of amazing things, even if you don't believe it yet.

"The world will be saved and remade by the dreamers."

SARAH J. MAAS

Contents

I

A Section on Relationships

Your Shoes

I still think about you sometimes.

Then, I was a child.
Now I'm not, but still,
I remember you.

I recall how I cried when you left;
tears of adolescent misunderstanding
stained my cheeks so
easily forgotten by you.

This wasn't new, though.
I wasn't allowed entrance
to your crew, *The Bandits*,
the siblings brigade I was
never a part of.

Perhaps I wasn't perceived as "sister"
when the two of you had
so much
in common.
You, the bumble

she, the bee.
I, the human the two of you sting,
the force that ends you
vehemently.

Somehow, though all this is true,
my mind ventures through time, and all I can see is
you.

You,
the actress who played sister *so well*
for *so long*.
We were the characters in your show,
though we never knew the cameras were rolling,
but Truman didn't either, I guess.
Neither of us asked to be a part of a performance.

And then, you called scene
but I wasn't ready for the credits to roll
or for you to leave home,
yet I, just a child, could do
nothing.

Your absence was a presence,
a tangible, invisible,
decay
that day by day
grew more distant.

In the width of your
remoteness,
when I could remember and recall,
I soon realized what you were is *not*

what a sister is supposed
to be.

Evermore, I try to fill the shoes
you never put on,
the soles tight from misuse,
but exactly in my size.
Yet, I sometimes
feel like they
still don't fit.

The Foundation

Driving in my car, eighty miles an hour, colors whirling past me through the windshield. I can't think straight, years seeming to fly past me in quick succession. I think of past loves, past heartbreaks. My childhood a cacophony of confusion—I couldn't hear, I couldn't understand, I *suffered*. Kids were mean (aren't they always?), and I was lost. Though, I always had a tether.

My parents. *They* were the buoy, the anchor, their love greater than anything else. Though, don't the people we aspire to be also have their own flaws?

Driving down the road, picking up speed, I am brought to a moment. Forced into it, my face being plunged into the cold waters of the past. I *see*.

Sitting on the hotel floor, racing suit on under clothes, bright blue UK hat warming my ears. It's race day, I'm ten years old—top of my age group—and I'm ready to win. My blood thrums, anxiously waiting for my parents to be done getting ready, to take me to the pool where for once, I am a kid that can fly.

"Are you almost done?" My dad calls to my mom, him yelling through the wall that leads to the bathroom. He's anxious, running numbers and stats through his head, preparing to coach me to greatness.

"Just about!" Mom says, excitement in her voice. My sweetest supporter, even when I touch the wall last, when the medal is bronze, when I'm losing.

My dad paces, his thoughts like toxic radiation, but I'm used to the buzz. I am made of it, this chaos. Both born and bred from it.

I look to my mother, the back of her tan arms facing me, and I watch as she finishes getting ready. The swift movements, the light air of hope for the day ahead. Joy for her daughter doing big things in a world she once could not face. She puts her makeup brush down and picks up some mouthwash, the movement a quick, subtle thing. It's almost time to go, and I'm ready.

"Where's my charger?" Dad mumbles, throwing blankets and towels off the hotel couch. He'll need it, of course, to incessantly check Meet Mobile, always watching the competition, how I stack up against them. He looks for it furiously, going to the bedside table, the desk, and finally, the bathroom.

My mother moves out of the way, spitting the mouthwash, saying, "It's right here," wiping her mouth with her hand.

He picks it up, letting out a sigh of relief, then looks at her. Stares just a moment too long, then says, "That makeup makes you look orange."

Dad walks out of the room, adjusts his glasses. "Are you guys ready? Warmups start in thirty."

Mom looks at him, lips tight, arms straight. A million words shine in her eyes, but this time, she says none of them. She looks at Dad's back, something in her face crumbling. She shudders, turning back to the sink.

I watch, rapt, as she wets a washcloth and wipes all the makeup away. She is fierce with each swipe—unspoken words in each movement. In the reflection, her tears shimmer, but they never fall. My mother is not one to let her children see her cry.

When she's done, she looks at the cloth, all her makeup staring back at her. She sits it on the corner of the tub, looks back up at herself in the mirror. There is an expression on her face I cannot decipher, but one day, when I'm in a car, driving eighty miles an hour with colors racing past, I will understand. I will recognize the solitude of this one single moment.

She turns to face us, putting it all behind her, and walks through the door. My dad never looks back. "I'm ready," she says, looking through us. "Let's get to the pool. You've got a long day ahead of you, honey."

She speaks, but I don't hear the words. For I am transfixed by the washcloth sitting on the bath's edge. The makeup on its surface. The story left untold.

Wendy Darling

She couldn't find her glasses.
I watch her like a ghost, her wrinkled hands
search through her purse, unpainted nails scratch
specs, but those that are for her
eternal-summer climate,
not the ones she's looking for.

She searches high and low,
into the kitchen she goes,
catching a whiff of the dinner that's cooking.
I watch her mind wander to the groceries on the counter,
practically hear her think:
I have to wash the grapes, the grandkids are coming,
so she turns on the water, cold drops gracing her hands,
only to realize she never found her glasses.

I hate that she did it again,
her mind running like a river,
similar to the one she
talks about
traveling with her boys
when they were younger.
But now they're older,

like weeds that won't stop growing,
and all she can say is *why couldn't there be Peter Pan?*

Her words sink deep, killing some part of me,
though I realize she doesn't even remember I'm here.
Truly, none of this was ever intentional.
For I know she wants to be like Peter,
with his power to keep life eternally youthful,
free of forgetting,
of overlooking,
of being
lost.

But alas, Wendy never could fight
the moving of time, the infinite churn
that takes her delicate mind with it.
I know she's tired of this,
but she'll never say it,
so I watch while her heart crumbles because
once again, she realizes her task has slipped
from her mind, swift as the glimmer of pixie dust in the air.

I steel myself for the worst, her unbecoming,
(*my* unbecoming)
but she only puts her head in her hands,
refusing to give up
—always stubborn to the bone—
knowing in the end she'll find her glasses,
knowing that won't stop this from happening again.

30

I found myself in a foreign place, with foreign faces, and foreign shapes. The world looked like a dream, like one of those movies we used to make.

Around me, the setting sun shines bright, the past grows dim, and I find myself alone. No longer am I running through the backyard chasing my sister, my friend, to all the unknown, secret places we had yet to find. To *create*.

In this foreign place, I look about me. I search for those little girls with an imagination and a determination that the world itself was forced to bend to all these years.

Girls that flew without wings, that sang when all was quiet, that ran when the world said walk. I look for them, those partners in crime, those deviants that are truly divine.

At first, I couldn't see them among the Earth's chaos. But these girls have never been the kind to blend in; no, they were born and bred and raised to stand out.

So now, while I stand alone, arms crossed and mind quiet, I see them. Out in the distance, they dance and sing and rage against the many colors of the setting sun, fighting for more light, fighting the final moments of their game. They never did enjoy stopping when time was up.

I take a step towards them, yearning to see the faces of those adolescent dreamers. I watch as the two girls made of flame and life and fury crash to the ground, a tumble of small bodies and big thoughts. Even from here, from this unknown place, with these unknown people and unknown shapes, I can hear the riotous laughter I have come to remember.

They pick themselves up, taking a running leap, never apart, but infinitely together. With the speed of unyielding time, they run and run and run into the distance, into the bright bright shine of the sinking golden sun.

I drop to a knee, an unexpected and misunderstood tear escaping. "Wait!" I yell. "Don't leave!"

The two girls don't listen, though. They keep running, evidently racing towards a destination I cannot follow. They grow smaller and smaller, slowly but surely fading into the vast colors of dusk.

I put my head down, refusing to look, to see the escape of a childhood dream.

But then I feel a hand, and I see a face made of familiar shapes.

I look into your eyes, and find that I am not the only one with tear-stained cheeks. You look at me, a smile filled with hope and love and all the things that have brought us here. You put your hand out, and I take it.

I always will.

With our hands intertwined, and the world long behind, we look into the distance. Far, far ahead, where the horizon meets the ground, and this chapter closes down, the two girls run, hands joined, into oblivion.

"Where'd we go?" I whisper, the words for you, and you alone.

"Right here," you say. "Right here."

I look at you then, and smile a smile that matches your own.

Then, with our hands together as one, we walk forward, a mirror of two other girls from another time and another place.

Our destination is unknown, and the story is unwritten, but throughout it all, one thing stands true:

Through everything, from dusk till dawn, when light turns dark, it will always be us.

Together.

II

A Section on Mental Illness

Vincit Qui Patitur

I Am

You see, I have these incessant thoughts,
thoughts even the medication can't slow,
with the speed of light swim my thoughts,
thoughts I can't, and never will, control.

My friend, yes, I do look normal,
normal I am anything but,
air bursting out from my seams: normal,
normal, my state of contrast shipwreck.

You know that my mind spins, spirals,
spirals like my sense of reality,
anxiety controlling my every whim; spirals,
spirals plural because that's all my brain knows.

Now, I'll give you a normal stanza,
though, this story is anything but,
for I am the tide that never releases,
the storm from out at sea,
I am the girl who rages internally,
I am OCD.

The Unseen Malady

No one was supposed to know that I have an invisible disease. I keep it to myself, ensuring that my friends and family, as well as my foes, do not see the cracks in my armor. Armor that I have been wearing to guard myself from the world since I was young, since I was a child with dreams that had never heard of such a thing called reality.

I have always taken pride in the way I hide my downfalls. Laughing as the girl with the shiny hair tells a joke, smiling as the boy recounts a story that we both know is untrue, always blending in with all the other faces, I portray myself as "normal." Even here in this club surrounded by swarms of people, no one can see that something about me is… off. That's the wonderful thing about having an illness that cripples you from the inside: if you choose, no one has to see you suffer.

No one has to watch as your mind whispers that everyone you love will die because of you, and the only thing you can do to save them is the *tap*

tap

tap

of your fingers. *That* will save them from greeting the land of which no mortal returns.

No one has to see you crumble from within while the voice that sounds oh so similar to your own intrudes when you are happy and smiling, only to tell you that you don't deserve that smile. Inside, the moment is ruined, but outside, no one else can see that your smile has gone from genuine to fake. The most lovely of facades.

No one has to know that you are a shell of a person, barely holding on to your sanity, always at the mercy of the monster that has made a home inside the collapsing walls of your mind.

I have lived this way for as long as I can remember. There may have been a time before I coexisted in my own being, but that time was too short-lived to have had any kind of impact. That's okay, though. It makes situations that I am in now far easier to bear.

It's roughly eleven o'clock, and the flashing strobe lights are a beam that illuminates the darkness, momentarily allowing me to see the people around me, seemingly hundreds of them inhaling and exhaling in waves. The light radiates off my dress, a black and sparkly thing that might look nice on my form. My hair curls around my shoulders, each strand a flawless spiral. I spent hours perfecting this small piece of me. In fact, I even went as far as choosing makeup to accentuate the color of my eyes, what might be perceived as natural beauty. Realistically, I know all of this holds no weight. Deciphering what I truly look like these days is difficult; my disease can tell me whatever it wants, and I will believe it.

But now I'm too distracted to care about how others may perceive me. I saw him across the floor of churning people, and now I'm floating in the sea of humanity that dance and sing to the music that fills the club, the bite of alcohol burning my nose as it sachets towards me from all directions. For me, there's no more dancing or singing or smiling. My thoughts are racing 'cause they've been triggered by the boy who is now a man, a man that was once a boy that found joy in deconstructing me. The floor is sticky, and I worry that I'll get stuck in my place here forever, the man that chewed me up and spit me out, an entity that hovers closer by the minute. Just ten feet away now. I'm still here, but he won't stop coming. *Please*, I beg my monster, *don't let me collapse now. Let me fight, let me win.* But then my mind whispers that it will all be okay, just close your eyes and *jump*

jump jump.

Those three small actions, the compulsion that I must pay heed to, will keep me pulled together. I try to push down the panic, refusing to cave to the impulse when so many eyes are on me, but it comes in waves, quick as anything I have ever known.

No, I scream inside the walls of thought that I am trapped in. I stumble on my feet and my friends sway around me, but I'm not dancing, I'm dying, I'm trying, but it's futile. In my heart, I know it is already far too late. I disobeyed my brain, refusing to respect that demented pattern of three. I can't, for the world would *see,* and my disease would take another piece of me. The piece called privacy, my little secret, the right to my hidden demise.

When I look back on this moment in the future, I will wonder why my armor chose this night to shatter into a million pieces. I will contemplate the catalyst of my unbecoming, forever questioning if I could have pushed back harder, keeping the beast at bay for just a *second* longer. I will try not to blame it on the man who was once a boy, the one that treated me as if I were a toy, but both me and my monster know that there will never be a concrete answer. Sick people can never see the moment that will kill them until it's already upon them.

Bugs are crawling under my skin, and I know that if I don't hide or escape or *something,* everyone in this raging pit of dancing ghosts will see me be condemned by the demons I share a brain with. That can't happen

that can't happen

that can't happen

because the man who almost seems like a mirror has seen the writhing insides of my monster once before and he's getting closer, just over my shoulder, and he *must* know that I'm wounded, that I'm bleeding, cause he's a shark that circles me and I know he knows I'm going down, faster and faster by the minute. The memory engulfs me, my body shakes, but my mind goes utterly still. When it makes me look and see, it must be silent, it must be still. This predator knows how to prepare their prey.

Don't you remember how you trusted him? That day you showed him your darkness. You unlocked the gates of our prison and showed him what it truly looks like here. For the first time, you allowed him to see the dark side of our duality. A tear slid from the corner of your eye as you thought, finally, someone truly *sees* me.

Yes, he did see you. He looked into your eyes, love and hope and wonder there, a living phantom. You brought your hand up to his jaw, strong and firm, just like all the rest of him. You brushed his skin with the pad of your thumb, still soft from years of calm adolescence. Soft like his hair, like his body underneath you, like his heart. Or at least how you perceived it.

"I loved you, Nichole. I really did. But you are sick. *How do you expect me to stay with someone that can't even look in the mirror? How am I meant to love someone who isn't in control of their own thoughts?"*

You see that his eyes are bleak, and his heart has turned fiery, the crazed red and orange volatile in their pursuit to burn you. We let you get close to the flames, knowing this is best for you, knowing we will use this to convince you to commit our compulsions far down the line.

He pushes your hand away and you start to turn in on yourself, waiting, watching, wondering why your love, your life, has gone as distant as all the far off places you don't dare travel.

"You are not the person I thought you were. I don't think I even know you at all."

His words cut you, didn't they? Yet you still responded. "I am no different than I was all those years ago! I was born this way, can't you see that? I have no control! I didn't ask for this monster to make a home in my mind; I never wanted to fight for a voice in my own inner monologue. Baby, it hurts and I hate it, but every day I fight against it. I will get better. I promise! Don't you love me enough to see me through this? After everything, don't you owe me at least the effort of trying?"

You should have known you would never win in a fight against us. He did. He knew.

You remember as well as us his face of stone as he turned his back on you, shoulders taut in anger, in loss. He opened the door, saying, whispering, yelling, "I cannot love those that are ill and unfixable. I refuse to call a broken girl mine."

Then I'm dropped back into the real world, my body still shaking, the people around me quickly closing in, but my mind is no longer still. No, now it races tenfold the speed it did before, and I must run, I must escape, for the world will see me collapse from within if I don't.

In a sentence that consists of an accordion of words that smoosh themselves together, I tell the group of girls I came with that I need to go to the bathroom. As I turn on my heel, keeping each compulsion inside, I tell the girls, no, don't come with me. Don't come watch me fall into a pit of spiraling madness; the spitting hell that I have learned to call home. I whisper internally, *hush, breathe, don't let them see,* attempting to soothe the panic that has already taken hold. My breath comes faster, and my feet become a wobbling mess as I rush towards the door. People look at me in anger and annoyance as I step on their feet, my pace barely below the canter of a run.

Another step, and the corners of my vision go dark, my peripheral now a double set of blinders. It makes me fear, for I cannot see the boy who is now a man, the shark that hunts what he perceives as lesser than. I swear I hear screaming and the intruder that lives inside me yells, "go faster!", so I do, I do, I do! I'm wheezing now and everyone is chasing me, pursuing me like hunting dogs hot on my trail. I snap my neck *left*

right

left,

because they tell me to. Now I'm too scared to disobey them, I refuse to put up a fight. There's a buzzing in my ears, and I think I'm getting closer to the door, because that's air in my face, and I hope it's not his breath, and I hope those aren't his feet that I'm stepping on, but maybe that's an illusion, a lie made up by my monster to give me hope when there is none,

when there is none,

when there is none.

I grapple for the handle of what must be the door, but I can't be too sure 'cause my vision's gone dark, but the voices got louder, and I think someone might be yelling at me, but I just can't quite be sure. I feel a cold burst of air on my face and I smile because I know I've finally escaped, and there might be a hand on my arm but I know it must have the intention of causing harm because my monster tells me everyone only ever wants to hurt, but you can save yourself, Nichole, you can. Just

step

step

step

and you will be free of the hand, you'll bear no scars, and that's the plan. Of course I listen, this will keep me safe, will keep everyone safe, so I take three great big steps. The arm is gone, but the air is moving fast around me, and I think I might fall, and there's yelling, and then there's something bright behind my eyes that are closed, and then I'm on the ground and there is no thought.

* * *

The smell of cleaning agents and the beeping of machines overwhelm me before I begin to open my eyes. Hushed voices surround me, so I muster up the effort to see what's going on. Upon opening my eyes, I find myself in a hospital bed, multiple machines sending data to some far-off computer. The doctor turns to me, hearing my movements as I assess my many small cuts and bruises that burn. I see his face, and in a blink, my body tightens up and the compulsions come calling; this man is a man I know, but I thought I had escaped him, all of him, but now he's here and now I hurt—

"Hello, Nichole; I'm Doctor Scott, and I can assure you that you are in good hands." He takes a step closer to me, holding a clipboard and pen. "Do you know why you're here?"

The man looks at me, and while I look closer, shut my eyes and listen to his voice, I realize he is not the one who haunts me. I take deep breaths, keeping the monster at bay. Opening my eyes, I shake my head no.

"You ran in front of a car, Nichole. If it wasn't for the security at the club you went to, you would be dead. They pushed you out of the way just in time, and you will be okay, but you need to be more careful next time. We're running tests right now, but I assume you just had too much to drink. There's nothing wrong with you; everything will be okay, aside from a few cuts and bruises. If you take good care of them, they won't last, either."

The doctor speaks to one of the silently working nurses, then makes for the door. Before leaving, he says, "Since you've suffered no real injuries, and assuming all the tests come back clear, you will be permitted to leave tonight. Feel free to contact anyone you like, and if you need, we can provide assistance."

With that, he walks out the door, leaving me with my thoughts and the silently working nurses. I assess the situation, contemplating how I got here, cut, bruised, and bleeding. I stare at the ceiling, heart beating its hollow rhythm.

I know I didn't have anything to drink. So does my monster. But there's nothing wrong with me, as the doctor said. Nothing that you can see. Nothing that matters; nothing that's real.

If he knew what I had living inside of me, I wonder if he would call me sick. I wonder if they would let me go, or make me stay in this place, too worried about the unknown, the possibility of my disease being contagious.

Not to worry, I would respond. My disease is invisible, my silent tormenter, unable to touch those around me. It will kill me before it ever touches another soul. They're deadly, the things that can hide in plain sight. The things that come out of hiding when triggered by a man or a memory, a fear or a fury. Perhaps what is most frightening is the fact that sometimes it needs no force of motion to set it on its warpath.

Sometimes all you have to do is breathe. Breathe and
breathe and
breathe.

Rocks Against a Wall

Rocks hit the wall, going nowhere, the sound enough to puncture the night.

I don't know how else to calm these thoughts, these great wars that are waged without consideration of my sanity.

These stones will break my bones, but the words that spit like fire left nothing to be broken. Words are a powerful thing, you see. They breed thought, and thought breeds hope, and hope is the most dangerous being of all.

It picks you up and tells you things are getting better,

they are they are they are,

but they **_aren't_**, yet you don't know that. You listen to those sweet honeyed words, you drink them in like the finest nectar, and by the time you realize the truth, the damage has long since been done.

So you throw rocks at the wall because you're sick of this, sick of this hopeless hope that you can't help but believe in, even after all the loss, the pain, the unbeknownst punishment, because to you, what else is there?

You let the *crack* fill the silence, your arm still stinging from the windback—the throw—and you know that hope is the worst villain of all. It let you believe you could have something good, truly *have* it; nurture it and love it, and for once, call it yours. But nothing ever comes at face value, despite what hope whispered in your ear.

You know that now, and the rocks in the night know it too.

III

A Section on Love

"To whatever end."
Sarah J. maas

Love is a Thorn

In response to Pablo Neruda's "One Hundred Love Sonnets: XVII"

*I love you as one loves obscure things,
secretly, between the shadow and the soul.*

You were my secret, my bloody oath,
palm cut and oozing into yours.
I lived and died by you,
our shadows intertwining,
two leashes becoming one,
tethering us.

I adored you between breaths,
between days and years,
each eclipsing night,
the moon casting our shadow.
Through that darkness, I delighted in you.

*I love you as the plant that doesn't bloom but carries
the light of those flowers, hidden, within itself.*

A cactus, you poked me,
destined to push me away.

Though, full of water, I soaked you up,
for I was a drought.

Your beauty, hidden behind spikes,
like knives, like words shaped as bullets.
Lovely, your violence,
living between bones.

I love you without knowing how, or when, or from where,
I love you directly without problems or pride.

Swallowed gum, grass growing in my stomach,
myth's origin untold, same as our beginning.
Where your blessings came from,
a great unknown, vast as the ocean,
deep as the darkest sea.

My infatuation is yours directly,
without hesitations or backward steps,
your eyes singed into my soul,
our love a sonnet still to be written,
read, and carried like weights.

Cold as Death

She was ice,
Nature's hatred,
the World's rage.

He picked, he played,
pursued both grace and glory.
Unaware of the alternative side
to her coin.

Chance after chance,
she offered him mercy,
the benefit of the doubt,
kindness she had never known,
denying herself her nature.

And still, he plotted.
Took advantage of the smiles,
the laughs, the gifts, all freely given.
He did not know this was a privilege,
not a right.

Mistreated, day after day,
their death hidden in delicacies.

He did not know what she could become.

And become, she did.

For she was ice, rage,
vengeance.
She hid her nature,
providing comfort,
providing calm.

Now, she has awoken.
Ice like glass surrounds them,
she smiles, eyes dark, smile bright,
for she had been underestimated once again.

Yes, she is a sweet little thing, of course,
but only when she wants to be.
She would not be played as a fool,
and a fool he had played her.

Now, all she had offered, given, extended,
is snatched into oblivion,
along with her kindness,
her heart.

Now she is cold,
she is stone,
she is stoic in the face of
lifeless apologies.
For him, she is a *ghost*.

We Are Found in Finalities

"This is the last time, and we both know it. Don't lie to me, please, that's all I ask."

I look into his eyes and realize we are meant to be a glimpse in time. I know this is the end of a fleeting moment, the last pixel of a greater image. I find I don't want to hold on, but instead, need to let go.

The two of us, holding onto something in the midst of collapse. A goodbye edged in earthquakes. A moment found in finalities.

"I am no fool," I tell him, "and neither are you."

One Month Before

Lights shimmer a thousand different colors—purple, blue, gold—and I soak them all in like an awe-inspired child. The world falls away with the music, "How Deep Is Your Love," Calvin Harris' best song raging through speakers I can't see but still know exist.

Alone, I dance, I sing, I relish the tidal wave of bodies that undulate around me. Everyone smells of alcohol or weed, but I ignore it, cherishing my eternal sobriety, admiring the fervent turmoil of these conniving substances.

Alone, I people-watch, seeing the girl kiss her friend, the jealous guy who's been buying them drinks, appalled. I laugh at the absurdity of it, the beauty of such a human thing. Couples dance and sing to each other, love in their eyes and movements, whilst others find someone to go home with, hating the idea of being alone.

Alone, how I stand as I see you with your friends, talking, laughing, smoking, having fun. I stare as you lazily bring the blunt to your lips, eyes hooded as you speak, and I never look away, not one to be scared of being caught looking. A smile pulls at my lips as I watch you laugh, enjoying this life as you should, so young and free as you are.

A crash to my left, and I look away to see a drunk girl fallen over, legs and limbs splayed, pink dress misplaced, too much fun for her body to handle. She laughs and her friend picks her up, and I smile at the sight of it, missing my own friends so many states away.

I swirl back around, enjoying the music alone, looking back to find you already staring.

Smiling, covering my mouth, I mess with the bottom of my red dress, a thing from Shein, all I can afford. I feel seen, deeply, by your eyes. Your friends sway around you, but you are the rock by which the water parts, standing still amongst them. You smile at me—such a beautiful thing—and I take that as an invitation to find myself next to you.

As I take my first step, so do you, and I laugh, excitement a glimmering aura around me.

You meet me halfway, and now we're in the middle of the dance floor, two people coming together as one amongst many. The music gets quiet in my ears as we take each other in. I can't imagine how you see me, so I don't even try. How could I, when I am so engulfed by you?

I look at you, your jeans and black t-shirt so simple, yet so perfect and so right. Your skin, a beautiful tan shade, your hands, worn down from years of hard work. Hair as dark as midnight, the black strands complementing the dark shadow of your beard. Big lips, a perfect nose, and of course, the eyes. They are brown, the loveliest brown, similar to the glass-like rocks by the sea, like the soil that gives life to all nature. Heavenly, those eyes.

We both realize we've been staring in the same breath, though it seems neither of us can manage to be embarrassed.

"Hi—"

"Hello—"

We both stammer and laugh, and I put a hand on your shoulder, breathing in your cologne.

"I'm Nichole. You are?" I ask, stopping us from talking over one another.

"Leo. Lovely to meet you, Nichole."

You grab my hand from your shoulder, bringing it to your mouth for a kiss, like butterfly wings on skin.

"Leo, your voice," I say, "you've got an accent, where from?" The words meet my lips, my hand still in his, our eyes locked.

"Mexico, Atlanta, a little bit of both," you answer, putting a strand of hair behind my ear.

I catch your other hand in my own, you smile at me, and for a moment, the music gets loud again, and we dance. The crowd is close yet distant, and all I can think about is you as your scent engulfs my nose.

The song ends, and I stop us, pulling you along with me.

"Let's go somewhere," I say, excited at the thought.

Your teeth glint in the purple, blue, gold lights, a wicked sort of smile, asking, "Where?"

Your beautiful brown eyes looking into me, I say, promising, "Anywhere."

We leave together, and today, I am no longer alone.

Hours later, the clock ticks by, but with you, time is standing. I learn of *you*, love what I grasp, and ask for more. You were raised in Mexico by your mother, your father staying in Atlanta, until at long last, you returned to the States. You tell stories with your hands, hands that build and break things, and I find myself entranced.

We walk down the river, finding a donut shop open late into the night, and we go in, hand in hand, sharing years that were not lived together.

You buy me a donut, and they fry it with ice cream in the middle. We sit by the water, laughing, enjoying each other, eating our donuts.

"It's way too sweet," you say, laughing.

"Of course it is," I respond. "The best things always are."

We eat and talk and laugh, enjoying every second of each other's presence. It is a beautiful thing, the sound of your voice.

Walking back down the river, plane lights flashing in the sky, listening to boats passing by, you grab my hand as we walk towards the entrance to my apartment, your tone changing.

"I have to tell you, Nichole, a quite unfortunate detail," you say, pain in your face and eyes, hand clenching around mine.

I stop in my tracks, taking your other hand in mine, wanting to take the sorrow from you, saying, "Tell me."

Your thumb grazes my jaw, my chin, my lips, your eyes taking in every detail.

There is only pain as you say, "I'm going back to Mexico in a month. My mother, my sister—I miss them dearly. Mexico is my home, and I must return."

The sentences sequester themselves in my soul, becoming something undeniable. Running my hands along your arms, thoughts swim in and out of consciousness, weighing themselves together. What might happen if I continue down this path with you, you with a heart of gold and iron. You, whom I know so much and so little of. Looking at you, the sorrow and life and loss in your eyes, I find myself knowing, truly, terribly, my decision.

"Then let's have the best month of our lives," I say, a bitter smile biting at both my lips and yours.

"A month to remember," you say, as I lead us to my home.

Days and weeks blend together, each moment filled with you. Each night is spent in my bed, your warm body holding mine close, worshipping my skin like a temple. In this world, there is sex, and then there is what we have. Something deeper, something that transcends both language, physicality, and time. Time we do not have, but yearn for.

Like people in true denial, we live as a couple, waking and sleeping as one. Trips to Freddy's—my favorite fast food place, which quickly became yours— late-night ice cream stops, even when it's too sweet for you, jokes held like hands. We traipse through restaurants, trying one of everything, our entire relationship an indulgence. We go to the mall, buying each other gifts, taking photobooth pics, acting like eternal kids. For this month, we are in love.

Forehead kisses that steal my breath, a fire that lights something once cold inside me. I learn you, you learn me, both of us wishing for eternity. Weeks run away from us, and we chase after them, as children chase birds on the beach.

There are things that I learn to love about you. Your laugh, so easy to love, of course, but even more, I cherish the peek of your slightly crooked bottom teeth that show when you are truly happy. I love the calluses on your hands as they graze my own, the proof of your hard work and dedication. I love the way you fall asleep to Spanish podcasts, smiling even as dreams take you.

Days wind down, and I get both angry and sad. I imagine you, sparkling on the dance floor, an image stuck in my head I'll never shake. Blood roars in my ears as I grow attached to your shine, a shine you cannot see or won't accept, both ideas equally frustrating. Pain as our time comes to a close.

"This is the last time," I would force out, "and we both know it."

Words like these would flow in fits of despair, wishing you would leave, praying that you wouldn't, not knowing which would hurt worse. The next day, you'd be there, holding me close, and I cherished it so much I couldn't stand it.

I realized I was bleeding to death while standing, hating a place for taking my person, knowing it was inevitable.

There is nothing like the moment when one knows everything is about to change. We both knew without saying that we were approaching our end. Of course, we were ending even as we began, but without words, this was our goodbye.

I held you fiercely, hating my beautiful and loathsome heart, wishing you the best while wishing that was me. We were a season changing, a year's end, a flower wilting at the close of its life.

"Live in the now," you said, your accent curling the words. "Promise me."

I looked into your big brown eyes, your beautiful smile; a picture worth keeping.

"Always," I whispered, holding your hands over my heart, forcing you to feel its beating. To feel the vitality of this moment, the end of this lifespan, the dregs of our days.

You'd go on, and so would I, but as I led you to the door, I wondered how.

How someone can walk into one's life and change it forever. How a temporary thing can be as good as gold, as great as a god, all-powerful.

Your eyes sparkle, mine shed quiet tears, and I knew then that I would always reminisce this. You; us. *Always.*

Turning to leave, you drop my hand, and cross the threshold. Closing the door, the past, this story, I stand tall. I am lucky to have known you, truly. I am grateful for this gift, this moment in time, this small ounce of eternity.

In my room, the radio plays quietly, a Calvin Harris song that will always remind me of you. Of time turning, of years never had. I imagine you smiling with your mother and sister, and I grin, feeling joy for your life. Bittersweet goodbyes, love lost, beautiful memories that will exist years past, exceeding the fading of time. Exceeding a farewell edged in flame.

Lullaby

Our kiss, first and last;
contemplate the difference,
the dalliances that led here.

Reminisce the beginning,
your eyes a sparked match
catching flame.

Tears stream down cheeks,
realizing that I am an
afterthought.

Hands touching skin
like fire,
now ash,
now decay,
now nothing.

You knew it was goodbye,
farewell,
adieu.
But I,
clueless,

MY HEART AN OPEN WOUND

was at your mercy.

My heart
offered on a platter,
thrown to the wolves
to be feasted and fed upon.

I, something to
keep you busy,
a race never-ending,
my beating heart in your palms.

All this time,
your mind perceived,
my love at war,
though, for what?
Truly,
I never even knew you.

The Myth I Made of You

There is a unique anger in being fooled. A hot flash across the skin, war raging through blood, thick and heavy. She had cared for him deeply, triumphantly, but truly, it was always just a game. A puzzle with missing pieces, something never to be completed.

But still, she felt and gave to him with all her raging color, loving and appreciating every last detail. When he was rude or flat, she'd look past it, as girls always do, because *that's* how much she cared.

When the sex was bad, all about him, her body a thing to be used at his disposal, when the texts started fading, his words losing color, she let it go. Because above all, she had seen his heart in small glimpses, and she desired to cherish it, to hold it in her hands. *That* was who she was: a woman who ignored the truth, who gave her all to someone who wouldn't have cared whether she lived or died.

She had told him once that if he hurt her, it would change things irrevocably.

And that, it had. She'd turned to ice, to winter, to things hard and cold. Not towards men, but towards *him*, for using her, for being worse than his friend that she had known first, for fitting the stereotype of the selfish boy. She had convinced herself he was different, lied to herself a million different ways. A siren in her ear, the mythical creature creating delusions so beautiful and lovely.

She wanted to find retribution, to be evil, cruel, and cunning. But alas, she felt she had nothing left to offer him. At long last, he was not worth her time. For she had nothing to offer his poor, sad self. Getting high to fill the void, having sex to pass the time, a guy who will never exist outside of himself.

And she was better than that.

So she'd walk away. She'd turn her back, a ghost in the night, and she'd forget. Because the truth was, she felt sorry for him. For she was something to behold, a piece of gold in a sea of silver, and he was a blind man walking. She knew he'd search, perhaps without knowing, for something good, something golden, for all his life. But never, not once, would he find it. And when he turns back, when time has passed and he finds himself empty, she will already be gone.

The Hunt

I, the fugitive of my own heart.
Piece after piece to the void,
your void, dear Orion, hunter of my being.

I, alone here, within this dark,
but I extinguished you myself, so why am I surprised?
I, the chosen fugitive, the no-good thief of
my *own* happiness.

I, as cold as death inside,
but still alive, though hunted by both you and I,
your stars can't pierce this dusk of mine.

Fight this eclipse if you like,
your shine won't prevail,
but neither will I,
for this hunt *can't* end tonight.

Goodbyes

In response to Dylan Thomas's "Do Not Go Gentle into That Good Night"

Not every goodbye is sweet. Some are cold, and others are resistant. Ours was a beast, a dragon that pulled against its tethers, fighting for each bloodied breath. Like us, little did he know the raging was futile. Little did *we* know we were always destined for destruction. A beast basking in its own flames, burned by this fire of our own creation. Us and the dragon, burning down to ash.

A goodbye edged in flame. Things never were so simple with us, were they?

Here I am now, reflecting on our hellos, thinking they were infinite. I thought this would be forever. And I tried, *oh*, how I tried.

For all it's worth, I did *not* go gentle into that good night. I raged against the dying of the light, but in the end, it could not save us. It could not save *me*.

The mirror reflects my tears, but I do not hear my wailing. I stuffed my ears with past promises, thinking they might repair the cataclysmic hole that is our absence.

The mirror laughs, glass shards shimmering as I shatter it into pieces, my blood a sticky thing that shines. Let's be honest, though.

I am the pieces.

At last, what more could I give? I gave it all, and now all I've got is this.

The pieces.

Yes, now you're catching on, darling.

This is just goodbye.

To Covet

She knew how deeply she could love him, felt it from the beginning, and she was absolutely terrified of it. She knew the clock was ticking down—the minutes easing by—that she could never have him. The reality hit her like a thousand bone-deep cuts, a million pieces of shrapnel wedged into her heart.

A spark of fire burned within her, a blaze she hadn't felt in so long, and before she knew it, she realized she would eventually have to relinquish the flames.

"Why, dear Earth," she cried, "Do you grant me a hundred flowers, only to drench them in rain?"

The Earth looked at her, tears in her eyes, hands in her hair, and It trembled. It rarely witnessed the depth of the human heart, the gravity of that painful, rage-filled hope.

"Because," the Earth said, *"The dream is in the drowning."*

Like Porcelain, Like Glass

He didn't really love her,
even though he tried.
Not truly,
not when it
c o u n t s.

She believed him at first,
his fine words like china
paraded around,
an heirloom—an award—not earned but
sorely won.

Then his actions fell upon her like stones:
Light at first, then
thick and
Heavy.
His ceramic trophies
crashed
to the ground,
and with it, her tightly held
<u>Compassion</u>.

On the floor,

her hands open,
bloody,
she lets herself
s e e.

He is on the floor,
hands red
—like hers—
clutching his shattered
ceramic *gold.*

<u>He never even looks her way.</u>

Realization slaps her in the face.
Its hand is rough,
calloused,
practiced
in the art of dishing out
R E A L I T Y.

With the same hand,
it helps her up.
Out of the broken plates and cups,
their significance to her like
a wordless book,
a wingless bird,
like *nothing.*

She walks to the door,
he lies on the floor,
and wrapped in his broken comforts,
he cannot see that she is leaving him.
That after all this time,

she is
<u>Done.</u>

She has questions,
she'll let herself cry.
But through it all,
she'll remember:

This was not love.

She was not his life,
his dreams,
his everything.
She was not
anything
compared to his
fine porcelain china.

In a while,
after days,
she would grow to accept
that to him, she was a filler of days,
a smile, a hug, some love
when it was
convenient.

In a while,
she'd get over it.
This pain,
these cuts,
his accidental cruelties.
Eventually,
she'd realize she was

worth <u>so much more</u>
than glass.

A Love Letter to Leo, the Sun to my Sea

I plunged through the earth, past the surface, deep into the sea. For years, I had been drowning. Searching for a buoy that did not exist, a tether to the corporeal world, the great living plane. I thrashed and turned, a constant hurricane, a ship sinking out at sea. I watched while fish swam together, their colors a cacophony of beauty and love. Me and the fish, our solitary lives made one.

Then, one day, everything changed. There was nothing special about this specific turning of time, or the pulling of tides. Perhaps that's what made it so unique. One moment, I was alone out at sea, drowning vehemently.

And then there was you.

At the water's edge, you dove deep, avoiding the fish and foliage of the sea, coming straight to me. You put your arms around me, strong and soft and capable, and you brought me to shore. In the sun, there was you, a statue of golden perfection. I looked at you in awe, your eyes new to mine, yet I felt as though I knew them for an eternity.

We walked, hand in hand, through sand and salty air, sharing space and time. Seconds spanned the length of years, and over that time, I grew to adore you. We were seagulls soaring through the air, rain on a warm summer's day, a dolphin grazing the surface, guiding everyone to look at its beauty.

After some time, there was a feeling that began to burn itself into my chest. It started when you kissed me, salty lips reminding me of my years out at sea, and I realized I recognized this feeling. It was like drowning—losing breath—yet, it was beautiful. I was falling into you, seeing our future, gasping for air, but instead of oxygen, what filled my lungs was *you.* I was sunburned by your shine, your vitality, the glow that filled my being in your presence. There was no hope in avoiding this, this unbecoming of composure, your fire burning my soul to ash.

And I didn't want to avoid it, this burn that spread beneath my skin. It stretched to my fingertips and toes, and at once, I found its origin. My heart beat ferociously, my mind hummed in anticipation, the realization hitting me like a wave.

After all this time, this pain, confusion, solitude, I was falling in love. I was falling for *you.*

Though, falling wasn't the right word. For the first time, I was so far from the fish I once called friends. Now, I was flying. For you gave me wings, and I'd swing from clouds, having no bounds, because this love was greater than gravity.

From the sky, I would cry, joy filled tears turning to rain, filling the sea I once occupied. My laugh was thunder shaking the world, and sitting in the sky as the sun, you watched. I didn't recognize you before, but of course, I had always known you, even if I had not welcomed your shine.

Day and night, we danced together, becoming friends with the moon and stars. I had come so far from the sea, and even though I had spent years drowning, the birds would still skim the clouds and ask, "Aren't you far from home?"

At first, I was still, as if struck, the wind slashing my skin. I pondered and prayed on the idea of a place called home, wondering if it was the sea or the sky or the far-off place I'd been born.

Your touch burned my skin as you held me, and in your glowing arms, I found my answer. I had discovered my home in your presence, your love becoming a destination I would always yearn for, never satisfied until reached. My home was your voice in my ear, your kiss on my cheek, your shine eclipsing a month's worth of rain. I loved these things about you, your perfect imperfections, your roaring riot of a soul.

"Thank you," I whispered into your brilliant fire. "For showing me that love can be found and freed, even from the depths of the sea, from which I drowned for years so deeply."

Our Skiff

Crash
Tender waves hit the shore,
and for the last time,
I am reminded of
you.

Beyond, out at sea,
our story sails off,
in that one-person boat set
to never stop,
turn back,
or wait and see if we are coming.

I walk along the sand,
I stare at our skiff
and for the first time,
I do **not** reminisce.
For those days were mere
delusions,
and I no longer wish for your stale illusion.

There are old cuts on my skin

from your past abrasions,
and I remember picking the scabs and
relishing the sting,
for at least in those moments I had
an <u>inkling of you</u>.

Now, I look at the time-crusted blood,
the shade of brown just like your eyes,
and I know I can finally say I'm glad it's over.
I no longer see you in the beauty,
but in the dust,
the detritus of our legacy.

The waves
crash,
the riptide pulls,
but with this,
<u>I am stagnant</u>.

A Villain is a Victim

"Look at me. Look me in the eye and tell me you never cared. I dare you."

She seethed and she spit, but he didn't even blink. They never did, she had learned. For centuries, she'd let her heart bleed before her, let her veins be run dry by men who disposed of her like ash on a used-up cigarette.

She screamed at him—words indecipherable, words like a storm—but he never wavered.

To him, she was nothing.

She realizes this, too, in an instant, in a pain-filled breath. For a moment, she wondered if that was what suffocating felt like. Choking on air, reality so smothering that no oxygen can pierce it. Her skin—made of steel—turned to glass before him. *He* had made her this way, and she hated every loathsome second of it.

She looked in his eyes, searched one last time for an inkling of *anything*. Some proof that she gave her heart up for something. But, as always, he was as the archives demanded. As the history books predict, those stories always finding a way to repeat themselves. She was heartbroken, beaten down, brutalized by yet another disappointment. She was everything and nothing, all at once.

She was rage, pushed on by a million wrongs, a millennium of maltreatment. She needed change, so she became it.

She was stardust, she was glitter edged in gold. She was better than this, than him, than them, all those people who carved another notch into her heart. She pounded the truth into herself, forced it down her throat, scourged it through herself like fire.

He was gone, like the others (was he ever really there?), and alone, she trembled with her own ferocity. She refused to be left again, to be lost to the world, to its brutalities. She was a beast to be bartered with, a burn on the bones of her foes. A fool she would be no longer, a slave to those who never cared to begin with. She would break the cycle, the turning of time leading to repeated loss.

She refused to let history repeat itself once more. So she turned to the world and spoke into it, deeply, deathly still.

"Look at me. Look me in the eye and tell me you won. I dare you."

A Maiden's Hearth

A Maiden's Hearth
Smoke in the air
embers dancing like
secret lovers,
broken promises
bitten
between teeth.

Breathe in ashes
the scent of
old perfume,
a curved smile on
chapped lips.
Her favorite word
whispered
in the smoke:

Vengeance.

Fabric ripped and cut,
lessons learned,
victories won.
Liquid dried
ruby **red** on

porcelain skin
as good as
dead.

Mistakes, betrayal,
all the same.
a heart was ripped,
for *that*,
they **paid**.

No sticks,
no stones,
just female rage,
and years of misery,
thrown on logs
to
burn
away.

Icarus and I

I learned the hard way what it is to live and die in the same breath. To be stabbed by each inhale, my lungs punctured again and again by the pain of what I had next to me just moments before. Oh, how I had forgotten that the most beautiful stars in your sky can be ripped away in a *second*, leaving nothing but a pile of memory-filled ash at your feet.

I never thought this light would die.

I lay in these sun-sparkling ashes, cursing the power of love, the power of souls and eternity and the ever-present pushing of time.

I curse the sun for taking what I've fought for, what I've earned, simply because I flew too close to the sun; like Icarus, my wings tumble and twist, a million feathers falling to the unforgiving earth, my heart cleaving in two—so much worse than before—the pain of my body hitting the ground *nothing* next to death that is your absence.

I scream in agony, not from my splintered bones, but from the holes you left in my being, the spaces that are supposed to be filled by *you*, my sun, my star, my everything.

Again, I curse the world for giving me this fight, this war that rages in my soul for the great loves of my life. For you, I would do anything; not even these broken wings could stop me from flying to save you.

Though, even now, I don't lose hope. The ashes from my beautiful, burned stars cloud my vision, but I swear, in my sky, I see a light.

An ember, a blaze, a burning thing called a dream.

Perhaps this light's not dead.

Perhaps, it just needs a fresh sky to shine under.

How the Sky Found the Sun

She didn't know she was incomplete.

The clouds were congested.
Expansive grey filled the sky,
Rain patiently waiting in the wings,
Ready to be released upon the drought.

But she knew she was wandering.

Yet, the rain would not come.
Instead, it rested in the sky
With pressure pushing ever downward.

She assumed she would always do so.

The Earth cries out in pain,
Needing the rain to free all her children.
The skies are stubborn, though;
Never have they cared for mercy.

Then, one day, her heart screamed something new and unfamiliar.

When all seemed lost to the world,

The sky,
The storms,
Finally came the slight drizzle of
Clouds' teardrops.

"In the soul of a stranger is where you will find your home."

This was not due to chance.
Truthfully, the sun started shining,
And the sky admired the effort it put in
To burn so bright for
All these millennia.

Her eyes fell upon him, and she knew her heart spoke truth.

As a result,
The sky opened up,
And down came the storm.
Now, no longer a drizzle, but a
Phenomenon of extreme forces.
The sky wasn't used to letting go of so much.

In his soul rested a piece of her own, the lost piece called home.

All the while, the sun smiled down on the sky,
Creating a rainbow full of the brightest colors.
The rainbow is an anomaly; its creation impossible
Without the tears of the sky and
The open arms of the sun.

Her home was named Ross.

The most beautiful calamity, *the two of them finally*

Together.

Acknowledgments

I owe deep amounts of gratitude to many people, and although I cannot name everyone, I will do my best to name a few. Those that are ot named, please know you still have a special place in my heart, and on this road that has led me here.

First, I want to thank my parents, Amy and Jon Dickinson. Throughout my entire life, they have supported me, no matter what I was pursuing. When I told them I wanted to study Creative Writing at college, they backed me with their full and unbridled support. I acknowledge that many parents would not have reacted the same way to that news, and I will forever be grateful for their unyielding love and dedication to supporting me in my dreams.

I would also like to thank my late grandfather, Jeff Dickinson. Throughout his entire life, he was a dreamer. He was an actor and a director, a jack of all trades. He was never able to read any of my writing, but I know he is somewhere, thriving in whatever afterlife is out there, cheering me on from afar. In that, I have no doubt.

I want to thank my sister, Karlie Jo Dickinson, for being my fellow adventurer in our adolescence. We grew up traipsing through creeks and woods, playing imaginary games, and fighting imaginary battles. My imagination was born in our childhood, in the years we spent pretending to fly. The flash fiction piece titled "30" is dedicated to her, and it will always have a special place in my heart.

I would also like to thank my best friends (you know who you are!), and also my therapist for helping me through some of the most difficult parts in my life. I wrote some of these pieces when I was in a very dark place, and without them, I do not know if I would be here today. My gratitude for them is unyielding.

Additionally, I would like to thank my college professors, peers, and supporters. The constructive criticism and encouraging words have changed my work for the better, and while it will always be changing and improving, I would not be able to publish this work without them. To my supporters, I thank each one of you. I would not be here without you.

Lastly, I want to thank everyone who has ever broken my heart. Conversely, while many of them never did much good for me, it inspired some lovely writing, and much of this anthology would not exist without it. All names have been changed, of course, but ultimately, both love and the loss of it are incredibly powerful things. For any of those men offended by what I have written, here is my response: I warned you not to hurt a writer :).

In all seriousness, thank you to all who took the time to read *My Heart an Open Wound*, and for coming with me on this journey; there will be many more to come. Stay gold, everyone.

About the Author

A

    Living in Louisville, Ky., Karson Dickinson has a BFA in Creative Writing from Spalding University, and she plans to one day get her MFA. In her free time, she cuddles her five rescue pets (one American Bully, and four cats!), and hosts two book clubs. Literature is her life, and she hopes to make even a small amount of change with her own writing.

You can connect with me on:

🌐 https://www.instagram.com/karson.dickinson